Ernie

JAMES SUTHERLAND

Chapter 1

"Please Dad," the little girl cooed in her sweetest voice.

"No."

"Pleeeese!"

"No."

"Pleeeeese!"

"No."

"Pleeeeeese!"

"No."

"Pleeeeeeese!"

Dad had heard quite enough.

"Martha," he said sternly "do you *seriously* think I'm going to let that dog back in the house after what happened yesterday?"

Martha Miller chewed her lip thoughtfully as she ran her mind back over recent events.

"Oh – *that,*" she shrugged, remembering. "I'd forgotten all about *that*…" A day is a long time when you are nine years old…

"Well *I* certainly haven't," Dad snorted. "That dog is a pest and a menace to society, and as such, is banned from the house until further notice!"

"But Dad," Martha protested, tears welling in her eyes "Ernie didn't *mean* to poop in your slipper!"

Dad looked at her with amazement.

"Really?" he scoffed. "So let me get this straight - you are suggesting that this *mutt* of yours was simply strolling through the living room minding his own business when a poop shot unexpectedly out of his bottom and, by sheer chance, happened to land in my slipper?"

Martha gave her left pigtail a thoughtful twiddle. She had to admit it *did* seem a little far-fetched. *Perhaps she should tackle the thing from a different angle...*

"Well," she said, a note of reproach in her voice "it wasn't Ernie's fault - you should have checked in your slipper before you put it on..."

This had Dad rocketing from his armchair with outrage.

"Oh – I *see*," he exclaimed "now it all becomes clear - the whole thing was *my* fault! How *silly* of me not to realize..."

Sensing that she might have said the wrong thing, Martha maintained a respectful silence.

"Well – I've certainly learnt my lesson," Dad continued sarcastically. "Oh yes – in future, I shall take great care to check *each and every* item of footwear for unexpected dog dirt before I put it on!"

Martha studied him warily. Unless she was very much mistaken, Dad was beginning to lose his temper. His face was turning that funny bright purple sort of colour, which was always a sure sign…

"I'm sorry Dad," she sighed. "I didn't mean…"

"Well I'm afraid 'sorry' just isn't good enough, Martha. I have made my final decision on the matter."

"But…"

"As I live and breathe, Ernie does *not* set foot in this house until further notice!"

And with these bitter words, his face now a deep shade of crimson, Dad snatched up his newspaper and stormed out of the room, slamming the door behind him with a terrific *BANG!*

"Hmmf!" Martha shrugged to the empty living room. Persuading Dad to allow Ernie back into the family home had been a *bit* trickier than she had expected. Yet she was a very determined little girl and had never been one to give in without a fight. Dad may have won the opening skirmish, but the *real* battle was yet to come…

*

Out in the porch, tucked up warm and snug in his basket with his rubber bone, Ernie had listened in on the debate with much interest. Although he had welcomed Martha's stout defence of his actions, she had been mistaken in one key detail; he *had* quite deliberately pooped in Dad's slipper. Having been told time and time again that he must, under no circumstances, do his business on the rug, the sight of Dad's tartan size tens nestling behind the sofa had presented him with a perfect alternative. *How was he to know that the old man would make such a fuss?*

The discussion in the living room having concluded with Dad's dramatic exit, the little dog turned his attention back to his bone. Ernie simply *adored* his rubber bone; it was his most treasured possession in the whole wide world and he rarely ventured more than a few yards without it. Once upon a time it had been smooth, shiny and yellow; now it was brown, dirty and badly chewed up, but in spite of this, it had lost not an ounce of its charm as far as he was concerned.

"Ernie!"

A deafening yell from somewhere out in the hallway made him shrink back in his basket; *Martha*. Having come from a rescue centre as a puppy, Martha was the only real 'parent' Ernie had ever known, and he loved her almost (though not *quite*) as much as he loved his yellow rubber bone. If she had one fault, however, it was that her vocal chords operated at just two volumes, *LOUD* and ***VERY LOUD***. Still, her appearance on the scene usually meant one of two things; either there was some tasty food coming his way, or he was about to go out for a walk.

Walks with Martha were always an adventure, with excitement and thrills guaranteed - quite unlike those he occasionally took with Mum or Dad, who simply dragged him along the same boring old route every day. Martha, on the other hand, liked to explore just as much as he did, and was more than happy to indulge him whenever he wanted to investigate the many fascinating objects and smells that he encountered among the pavements and hedgerows of the village.

Seconds later, the door of the porch opened and Martha strode in, Ernie rising to greet her with his usual ecstatic *woof*, his tail wagging frenziedly.

"Hiya," the little girl grinned, giving him a playful tickle behind the ear "shall we go out in the garden for a bit?"

Signalling his consent with a *yip* of glee, Ernie scampered back over to his basket to fetch his rubber bone before following her along the corridor and out through the back door, wagging his scruffy tail madly as he went.

*

At the sound of a rumble of thunder over the distant hills, Martha looked up at the sky with a worried frown.

"Looks like rain," she sighed. "Come on, Ernie - we'd better go back inside."

Ernie looked at her in stunned amazement. *Go back inside? Was she joking? No way was he going back inside! How could Martha, an apparently sensible girl, for whom he had always had the utmost respect, come out with such an utterly ridiculous suggestion? Did she not understand that a game as serious as 'Chuck the Bone' was not something that could be abandoned for the sake of a mere drop of rain?* It was thus with an air of mild reproach that he picked up his rubber bone, trotted back over to where she stood, and dropped it at her feet.

"Ok," the little girl shrugged, casting another anxious glance towards the heavens "but this will have to be the last throw..."

Woof! Ernie assented with a frantic wag of his tail. *He knew she would see sense...*

"Are you ready?" Martha grinned, waving the bone tantalisingly above her head. "As it's the last one, I'll make it the biggest throw ever!"

In later years, whenever he reflected on the episode that came to be known as *The Rubber Bone Tragedy,* Ernie would be forced to admit that getting his owner to throw his bone one last time had been a grave error. Martha, he should have known, was not the sort of girl who did things by halves, and if she promised the *biggest throw ever*, this was precisely what she would deliver. At first, as he watched his beloved toy whizzing through the air, it seemed to Ernie that all was well. True to her word, Martha had executed a fine, arcing throw that seemed destined to land smack bang in the middle of the compost heap at the bottom of the garden. Rummaging in the compost heap was one of Ernie's favourite pastimes, and the thought of retrieving his bone from such a splendid location filled him with excitement. *But wait... What was this? His bone wasn't going to land in the compost heap... No - it was sailing high*

*above it... High above the compost heap...
And into next door's garden!*

"Whoops!" Martha giggled as she turned to head inside. "Never mind – it was only an old bone anyway. Come on – let's get in quickly before it starts to rain."

Ernie, however, did not move. Instead, he merely sat, goggling in wide-eyed horror at the section of fence behind which his bone had just vanished. He did not notice the menacing growl of thunder above his head, nor did he heed the first heavy raindrops as they splashed on the end of his nose. *His bone was gone... His beloved bone to which no other bone could ever hope to compare had passed out of his life forever and ever!*

Or had it?

Chapter 2

"Come on, Ernie, eat up" Martha spoke with a tinge of anxiety as she pushed the food dish closer to the little dog's basket "they're *Bingo's Beefy Bites* – your favourite!"

Ernie frowned at the dish and gave it a disdainful sniff with his little black nose. The loss of his rubber bone had sent him into a state of mourning so deep that even *Bingo's Beefy Bites* had lost their appeal.

"Goodness me," the little girl sighed "you've hardly touched a thing for two days now! If this carries on, we'll have to take you to see Mr Pickles, the vet, and you know how much you hate going to see Mr Pickles."

Ernie considered this. In stating that he hated going to see Mr Pickles, Martha was quite correct; this was a man who prodded and poked at him, who made him swallow foul medicine, and who had even once had the downright nerve to stick a needle in his bottom! His owner was totally mistaken, however, if she believed that *any* threat, however dire, would induce him to eat so much as a morsel of food until his bone had been restored to its proper place at his side…

*

Ten minutes later, seated at the breakfast table, Martha addressed her parents through a moody mouthful of cornflakes.

"Guess what," she munched "Ernie wouldn't eat his breakfast again."

"Oh?" Dad, scanning his newspaper for last night's football results, showed very little interest in Ernie's eating habits.

"Yes – he's been like this ever since he lost his bone."

"Has he really?" Dad shrugged. "Well I'm sure he'll snap out of it sooner or later."

Martha, however, was not prepared to let the matter rest.

"Maybe we should go round and knock on Mrs Wiseman's door and ask her if we can have it back."

Reluctantly, Dad lowered his paper.

"No can do, I'm afraid," he said, shaking his head. "I thought we told you – Old Mrs Wiseman had to move out a few weeks ago. She was getting very frail, so she's gone to live with her daughter."

The little girl frowned. This was genuinely disturbing news; Old Mrs Wiseman had been a nice lady who had, for many years, maintained an unwavering policy of dishing out toffees whenever hers and Martha's paths had crossed. *With Mrs Wiseman out of the picture, a new supplier of toffees would need to be sourced without delay...*

"Well, if the house is empty," she answered thoughtfully "perhaps we could just climb over the fence and get Ernie's bone."

"Oh no," Dad shook his head "it's not empty. Someone else has moved in – a guy by the name of Grimshaw."

"Well - perhaps you could ask him if we could have it back," Mum chipped in as she joined them at the table.

"Ask *him*?" Dad snorted, almost choking on his cornflakes. "Are you serious? Have you seen the guy? Why – he must be nearly seven feet tall…"

"But…"

"Shaved head, tattoos all over him, muscles like the Incredible Hulk…

"But…"

"No, Martha - if you think I'm going to knock on that monster's door and ask if he fancies joining me for a game of *hunt the rubber bone* in his back garden, I am afraid you are very much mistaken!"

Mum turned to her husband with a hint of reproach.

"Of course, if you're scared of him…"

"Oh no," Dad lied, his cheeks pinkening slightly "don't be silly, Claire. Of *course* I'm not scared. I just don't want to… to *disturb* him, that's all. I'm sure he's a very busy man."

Mum was about to reply, however when she looked up, she saw only an empty space at the table where her husband had been. The slam of a car door in the driveway, quickly followed by the revving of an engine confirmed that he had fled the scene and was on his way to work.

"I have an idea," she said, turning her attention back to Martha who was toying at her cornflakes with the same apathy as that which Ernie had displayed towards his *Beefy Bites*. "How about I give you some pocket money and you can call at the pet shop on the way home from school and buy him a new one?"

Martha twiddled her spoon thoughtfully at the suggestion. While Mum's scheme certainly had its merits, it suffered from one fatal flaw; Ernie, she suspected, would only be satisfied by the restoration of *his* rubber bone. Any replica, be it the shiniest, most expensive rubber bone in the universe, simply wouldn't do and would be treated as a rank impostor. *Still s*he told herself *in a crisis as serious as this, anything was worth a try...*

"Ok Mum," she sighed, hopping down from her seat "I expect five pounds should be enough."

"*Five pounds?*" Mum gasped, fumbling in her purse. "That seems like an awful lot of money for a rubber bone, Martha. Are you *sure* they cost that much?"

"Positive," the little girl grinned, snatching the note "*everything* costs a fortune these days. At least that's what Dad always says…"

*

As lunchtime approached, with Mum and Dad at work, and Martha at school, Ernie trotted down the garden path, his scruffy features set in a look of fierce and steely determination. Earlier that morning, he had conducted a thorough survey of the fence that separated his own garden from that of the next door neighbour, and in doing so had discovered a loose plank down at the far bottom corner, behind the compost heap. It must, he concluded, have come loose during the winter storms, and would provide a perfect opening through which a dog of his slight stature could comfortably pass. The garden on the other side of the fence represented mysterious and uncharted territory to Ernie, and the thought of the dangers that might await him there filled him with a nameless dread. And yet he knew that he had little choice; *if he ever wanted to see his beloved rubber bone again, he would have to brave the unknown, whatever the risks may be.* His mind made up, he crept forward and nudged the loose plank to one side with his little wet nose.

"I wouldn't go in there if I were you."

The sound of a shrill voice piping up behind him startled the little dog, sending him rocketing skyward in terror. Spinning on his heels, Ernie was astonished to discover that he was being addressed by a small, somewhat mangy-looking mouse from its perch upon a rusty old wheelbarrow.

"I b... beg your pardon?" he quavered.

"Allow me to introduce myself," said the mouse. "Montgomery's the name. I merely remarked that I would strongly advise against your going through that hole in the fence."

Ernie peered at the dark opening with growing alarm.

"Oh?" he trembled, turning his attention back to the tiny creature. "But my rubber bone's in there, you see, and I just thought I'd pop in and get it back…"

"A rubber bone, eh?" Montgomery shook his head. "I'm really not sure it's worth risking certain death for the sake of a rubber bone."

A cold chill coursed down Ernie's spine.

"C… Certain death?" he croaked. "W… What do you mean by that?"

"Oh yes," the mouse continued. "If you crawl through that hole, I very much doubt you'd survive for more than a few minutes."

This was definitely not the kind of thing that Ernie wanted to hear.

"B… But why?" he gulped. "Surely there can't be anything *that* bad in there."

"Oh, but I'm afraid there is," Montgomery squeaked from his perch upon the wheelbarrow. "There's a dog. Or, to be more precise, a *big* bulldog."

Again, this was bad news for Ernie. As a *small* dog, he had always been rather afraid of big dogs. They were just so… *BIG!* For a few seconds, he fell into a gloomy silence as he considered the position of affairs. Then a thought occurred to him.

"Just because he's big, it doesn't mean he won't be nice," he said, his furry face brightening. "Sometimes big dogs are the friendliest of all."

"Oh no," the mouse shook its head again, dashing his hopes in an instant "not this one."

"Oh?"

"No, my friend – I'm afraid he's not in the *least* bit friendly."

"Oh dear!" Ernie quivered.

"Indeed," Montgomery continued "it's fair to say that he's a nasty piece of work - one of those vicious, snarling blighters, all slavering jaws and gnashing teeth – you know the sort. As a matter of fact, *he's* the reason I've had to move house."

"Really?" Ernie quivered some more.

"Oh yes," said the mouse. "I *used* to have a lovely cosy place under Old Mrs Wiseman's shed, but thanks to him I've been forced to find alternative accommodation underneath this wheelbarrow."

The little dog's eyes widened with worry. "Why?" he gulped. "What happened?"

"Oh nothing much," Montgomery sighed. "He spotted me in the garden the other day and just happened to mention during the course of our conversation that if he ever set eyes on me again, he would chew me up into a sort of fine mincemeat before swallowing me in a single gulp."

"Yikes!"

"Yes," the mouse nodded in agreement. "Downright unfriendly, if you ask me."

A nervous silence ensued as Ernie's vivid imagination conjured up images of the terrible beast that lurked on the other side of the fence. But then a further image popped into his head, one which banished all of his fears in an instant; he pictured that very same terrible beast chewing on *his* rubber bone! Big dog or no big dog, this was simply unacceptable; the bone *had* to be retrieved at all costs. *What was the point of having a future anyway, if the future in question did not contain yellow rubber bones?* And so, with his steely courage flooding back in spades, Ernie puffed out his little chest defiantly and turned once again to the mouse.

"Thank you for your warning," he said "but I fear I must go. If I do not return, at least I will have perished in the noblest of causes. Goodbye, my friend – perhaps we shall meet again some sunny day…" And with these brave words, he scampered over to the hole in the fence and disappeared through it.

"Very well," a squeaky voice called after him "but don't say I didn't warn you!"

Chapter 3

"Pink's no good." Martha stood at the counter of the pet shop, scowling ferociously at Mr Longbottom, the owner. "It's got to be yellow."

"I'm very sorry," the portly bald-headed man replied, struggling to keep his cool "but as I have already explained, we've sold out of yellow bones and our next delivery isn't due until Friday."

"*Friday?*" the little girl gasped in horror. "That's *ages* away!"

"It's the day after tomorrow."

"But I've already *told* you," Martha pleaded, turning the ferocity of her scowl up a notch "Ernie's gone off his food 'cos he's lost his yellow bone!"

The shopkeeper, who had been having a bad day even before this little pipsqueak entered his life, had heard quite enough.

"Now listen here, Miss…" he said through gritted teeth.

"Miller – Martha Miller," came the spirited reply.

"Well, Miss Miller - I have clearly explained the situation regarding our stock of yellow rubber bones..."

"Yes but..."

"If you find this to be unacceptable, then I would politely suggest that you take your custom elsewhere..."

"Yes but..."

"However, if you wish to *try* your dog with a pink bone, I am prepared, given the circumstances, to offer you a small discount."

The mention of a discount caught Martha's interest.

"Oh?" she said, her eyes narrowing. "How much?"

"They usually cost three pounds, but you can have it for two."

Martha gave her left pigtail a thoughtful twiddle as she considered the offer.

"I've only got a pound," she replied finally "and I still think even *that's* too much for that rotten old pink thing."

Growing ever more flustered, Mr Longbottom gaped at the little girl, searching her steely blue eyes for any sign of weakness but finding only stout defiance. He was a beaten man and he knew it…

"Here," he groaned, pressing the bone into an outstretched grubby hand "you can have it for free – just please leave me alone!"

"Hmm, I'll *try* it, I s'pose," said Martha "but if Ernie doesn't like it, you can bet I'll be back here first thing on Friday…"

"Very well," the poor man gibbered "whatever you say."

"Provided he hasn't *starved* to death in the meantime, that is," Martha added darkly as she turned to march out of the shop "and *then* you'll be sorry…"

As the door slammed with a terrific *BANG!* Mr Longbottom mopped his shiny forehead with a mixture of relief and dismay. *When he had decided to pursue a career as a shopkeeper, he had never expected his life to be quite as stressful as this…*

*

His heart beating like a hammer, Ernie crept as quietly as he could through the thick undergrowth. In recent years, Old Mrs Wiseman had been too frail to look after her garden properly, and as a result the grass was waist-high and the paths and paving stones barely visible beneath a dense tangle of weeds and brambles. To a dog of Ernie's modest proportions it was not unlike the jungles of the Darkest Congo; *how on earth would he ever find his beloved bone in a place like this?*

*

"Tumty tumty tum," Martha sang boisterously to herself as she skipped up the steps and through the front door, flinging her school bag down in the porch.

"Mum," she hollered "I'm home!"

"Yes dear," Mum sighed, appearing at the kitchen door. "I thought I heard you come in. Did you have a nice day at school?"

"Not really," came the honest reply "it was dead boring. Where's Ernie?"

"I think he's out in the back garden, dear. Please don't march through the hallway in those muddy shoes.

"I stopped at Longbottom's and got him a new bone," Martha bellowed, marching through the hallway in her muddy shoes.

"Ooh," Mum smiled "that's good."

"Except it's a pink one," the little girl roared as she opened the door that led to the back garden "and I'm not sure if Ernie likes pink."

"Well dear, you never know. Perhaps he'll…"

BANG! went the back door as Martha marched out into the garden in search of her pet.

*

Ernie had not travelled far through the undergrowth when he became aware of a curious sound up ahead. He froze, listening intently, one ear cocked; *snoring.* Intrigued, he sat up on his hind legs and sniffed the air. *What was that? Could it be true? Yes - it was but the faintest of whiffs, yet there was no mistaking it... Ernie had picked up the scent of his bone!* With a *yip* of delight, the little dog bounded forward, his heart filled with joy at the prospect of being reunited with the love of his life. Indeed, his excitement was such that he forgot all about his conversation with Montgomery, and it was only when he emerged from the undergrowth that the mouse's dire warnings came back to him. Directly ahead, there was a stone patio, in the corner of which there stood a large dog's kennel. Worse still, judging by the snoring coming from within its walls, this particular large dog's kennel was clearly home to a very large dog.

Silently, stealthily, Ernie crept forward to investigate. Sure enough, sprawled fast asleep, with just its head and front paws protruding from the kennel, he discerned what was, without any shadow of a doubt, the biggest bulldog he had ever seen. And nestled snugly between those paws, those terrible, bear-like front paws, lay his beloved bone! Hardly daring to breathe, Ernie crouched, still as a statue, as he considered his next move. As he saw it, there were two factors which might work in his favour:

Factor 1: The beast was, at least for now, fast asleep.

Factor 2: His bone was nestled *between* its paws, not *underneath* them. *If he was very, very quiet and very, very careful, Ernie felt sure he could extract it without disturbing the slumbering brute.*

And so, still holding his breath, he stole forward until he was close enough to read the brass name tag on the collar that hung around the monster's neck. *Max* it said. *Now was the moment of reckoning*; slowly, delicately, he reached out a front paw...

"Ernie!" a familiar voice bellowed from somewhere back in his own garden.

The little dog paused. *Drat! It was Martha, back from school already...*

"ERNIE!" the voice sounded again, even louder this time.

Max stirred and let out a great yawn, revealing a fearsome set of fangs; fortunately, his eyes, for the time being, remained tightly shut. In sheer desperation, Ernie grasped at his bone with a quivering paw and gave it a gentle tug. *A split second longer and he would have it! If only Martha would keep quiet...*

"*EEEEERRRRNIEEE!*" came the ear-splitting roar from the other side of the garden fence.

Frozen to the spot, his outstretched paw still resting on his beloved bone, Ernie could only goggle in silent horror as Max let out another tremendous yawn before slowly opening one sleepy, bloodshot eye...

Chapter 4

Through the course of his short life, Ernie had found himself in many an awkward situation. The time when he had chewed Dad's brand new *Nike* trainers to a pulp was one that sprang to mind. *How was he to know they'd cost a hundred and fifty pounds?* Then there was the occasion when he had inadvertently peed on Mum's laptop. *Again, hardly his fault - if they went leaving things lying around on the living room floor, what did they expect him to do?* On both occasions, he had been caught red handed (or red-*pawed*, to be more precise) and been punished accordingly. Neither of the above, however, was anywhere near as awkward as his current predicament. There is, you see, a firm code of conduct among dogs under which it is strictly forbidden under *any* circumstances to steal the bone of a fellow canine. It is seen as dastardly and taboo – an abominable crime that only the vilest of villains would ever *dream* of committing. *'Yes,'* you cry *'but Ernie wasn't actually stealing the bone - he was only trying to get one back that already belonged to him.'*

Yes, reader – but, whilst this is undoubtedly true, the problem was that Max clearly was not aware of this fact. As far as *he* was concerned, the yellow rubber bone that he had found in his back garden earlier that day was his and his alone, and he therefore took great exception to the sight of this sneaky little thief attempting to steal it from him.

Hastily withdrawing his paw, Ernie knew he would have to think, and think quickly.

"Oh - hello there neighbour," he gurgled. "Lovely day, isn't it?"

"Grrrrrr!"

"I… I must say, it's very nice to meet you. My name's Ernie – I live at the Miller's house next door."

"Grrrrrrrr!"

Somewhat rattled, the little dog retreated a few steps and studied his adversary. This 'Max' seemed to have a very limited vocabulary, and it was clearly not going to be easy to strike up anything resembling a civilized conversation. *Perhaps he ought to try a more direct approach…*

"I'm terribly sorry if I've disturbed you," he said in a polite, yet firm, voice "but I was wondering if you might be kind enough to let me have my bone back."

This drew an immediate response from Max, though it was not the kind that Ernie had hoped for.

"My bone!" he growled, slapping a huge paw down on the rubber toy as if to underline his point.

Hmmm Ernie thought to himself. *This is going to be even trickier than I thought...*

"Ah yes," he nodded gravely. "I quite understand why you might *think* it belongs to you, but it's actually one of mine that just happened to be thrown into your garden by accident. My owner, Martha, you see..."

"My bone!" the massive dog repeated, rising menacingly up onto its haunches.

Ernie sighed. He had hoped to retrieve his property through peaceful diplomacy, yet it was becoming increasingly obvious that this was not to be. And so, with the air of a grownup addressing a naughty child, he puffed out his little chest and addressed the bulldog in his sternest voice.

"Now look here," he woofed "I don't want any trouble, but I demand that you give me my bone back right this minute!"

Max looked at him with a puzzled expression which quickly changed to one of amusement.

"Or what?" he growled with a smirk.

A simple enough question, you might think, yet it was one which had Ernie completely baffled. *If this monstrous brute flatly refused to give him his bone, what, in actual fact, could he do about it?*

"Or... Or else," he gulped "y... you shall have to face the consequences!"

Max frowned. Though he did not understand what *consequences* were, he *was* intelligent enough to realize that he was being threatened. And not only was he being threatened, but he was being threatened by a jumped-up little pipsqueak less than half his size. After a brief moment of consideration, he responded as any self-respecting bulldog would; with a blood-curdling roar, he coiled his muscles and made a sudden spring at his tormentor. Frozen to the spot with sheer terror, Ernie could only shut his eyes tightly as he awaited his ghastly fate. *Could anyone save him now?*

*

At that precise moment another roar of a similar volume could be heard in the hallway of the Miller household.

"MUM!" Martha bellowed up the stairs.

No response.

"MUUUUUUM!" she repeated, twice as loudly as before.

On the upstairs landing, a door flew open and Mum came hurtling down the stairs, almost breaking her neck in the process.

"Martha!" she cried, crouching to examine her daughter. "What's wrong? Are you hurt?"

Martha gave her a quizzical look.

"'Course I'm not *hurt*," she shrugged. "What makes you think I'm hurt?"

"Then why were you screaming up the stairs like that?" Mum gasped.

"I wasn't *screaming*," came the simple reply. "I was just *calling* to ask if you'd seen Ernie."

"Ernie?" Mum shook her head in bewilderment. "I was upstairs on the telephone to your Uncle Brian. Why would I have seen Ernie?"

"I just thought you might have, that's all," Martha scowled.

"Well I haven't," sighed Mum. "Now if you don't mind, I'll call your uncle back and let him know everything's ok. He must be wondering what on earth is going on."

But Martha wasn't finished yet.

"Never mind calling Uncle Brian - p'raps you should call the police instead."

Mum paused halfway up the stairs.

"The police?" she frowned. "Why on earth would I want to call the police?"

"Well - what if Ernie's been kidnapped?" Martha replied earnestly.

"Kidnapped?" Mum was growing more bewildered by the second. "Martha – no self-respecting kidnapper would want to steal a dog like Ernie…"

"Oh?" the little girl retorted, offended. "Why wouldn't they? Ernie's a very nice dog, I'll have you know, and…"

"Yes, but he's not an expensive pedigree, is he?" Mum interrupted, continuing on her way up the stairs. "Anyway – I'm sure he'll probably just be snuffling about down in the compost heap like he usually is."

"He isn't. I've checked."

"Well I'm sure he'll turn up sooner or later. Now, for goodness' sake – go outside and get some fresh air!"

Chapter 5

Long ago, when he was but a mere pup, Ernie's mother had told him about something called *divine intervention*. It was, she explained, a kind of unseen, magical force that had a habit of saving the day at the very moment when it seems like all hope is lost. As he crouched, fully expecting to feel the bite of the huge dog's teeth upon his person, Ernie was surprised to hear only a strangled 'yelp!' *Could it be that the good old hand of divine intervention had stepped in to rescue him in his hour of need?* Blinking open one frightened eye, he quickly saw that it had done nothing of the sort; Max, he now realized, had been tied to his kennel with a stout metal chain all along, and it was this chain, rather than any divine intervention, that had yanked him backwards, mid-leap, and deposited him in an ungainly heap on the concrete patio. Observing his stricken foe, Ernie briefly wondered whether it might be worth a stab at reopening negotiations about his bone, however the sight of Max beginning to stir quickly made him abandon the idea; the chain, though fairly sturdy, was a decidedly old and rusty-looking affair which could not be relied on to restrain the brute forever. No – just as Martha had done in her earlier battle with Dad, he would beat a tactical retreat and resume hostilities at a later point when the odds were more in his favour. And so, with a light *yip* of defiance, the little dog turned tail and scampered hurriedly away through the undergrowth.

*

"There you are!" Martha grinned as she spotted the small, furry figure trotting up the path. But as Ernie drew nearer, her grin quickly turned to a frown of dismay. "Goodness me," she gasped "look at the state of you! What on *earth* have you been doing?"

Ernie gave her a blank look. Perhaps his ordeal with Max had left him looking a tad scruffier than normal, but he had far more important things than appearances on his mind at the moment.

"Woof," he replied with a somewhat half-hearted wag of his tail.

"Never mind," said Martha, giving him an affectionate tickle under the chin. "Come along with me – I've a special surprise waiting for you."

Moments later, the little dog found himself being ushered into the porch where, nestling in his basket, he noted a mysterious object, carefully wrapped in gift paper. Though he could not guess what it could be, there was something about its size and shape that seemed oddly familiar. Approaching it warily, Ernie gave it an exploratory sniff with his little black nose.

Mmmm he thought to himself. *I'm sure that reminds me of something...*

Then it came to him; *it was the scent of rubber or, to be more precise, the scent of a rubber bone! Somehow, impossible though it seemed, Martha had magically retrieved his beloved bone and put it back in his basket where it belonged!*

His heart racing, Ernie goggled at her in awe.

"Well," Martha laughed, "aren't you going to open it up and see what it is?"

Ernie needed no further encouragement. With a *yip* of unbridled glee, he seized the paper package in his teeth and tore into it like a dog possessed.

*

Through in the kitchen, Dad had arrived home from work and was busy making himself a restorative cup of tea when Mum entered the room.

"Hiya," she said brightly. "How's your day been?"

"Alright, I suppose," Dad huffed. He had recently acquired a new manager in the office, a fellow by the name of Simpkin, whom he disliked intensely, but whose company he was forced to endure for eight hours a day; for this reason, Dad was rarely in the best of moods by the time he got home from work. "How about you?"

"Not too bad," Mum sat down at the table opposite him. "Martha seems in a funny mood, though – even grumpier than usual!"

At this, Dad shuddered visibly, almost choking on his tea.

"Grumpier than usual?" he spluttered. "But surely that's impossible!"

Mum took a deep breath. She knew that what she was about to say wouldn't please her husband, but she was determined to voice it anyway.

"I've been thinking," she spoke in her breeziest voice "that perhaps we're being a bit hard on her."

"Hard on her?" Dad gave her a puzzled look. "What do you mean, *hard on her*?"

"Well – I mean this business of banning Ernie from the house. Martha hasn't actually done anything wrong and she likes having him on her knee when she's watching TV in the evenings."

As expected, her remark went down like a lead balloon.

"Really Claire!" Dad snapped, rising from his chair. "I thought we were both agreed he'd have to stay in the porch."

"Yes but…"

"After what he did to my slipper…"

"Yes George, but it was only an accident…"

Dad, however, was in no mood to listen.

"Sometimes I wonder what the world's coming to," he huffed, shaking his head in dismay. "Everyone you meet these days seems to be obsessed with dogs. Anywhere you try and go – any street, any park, any beach, there are dogs, dogs, pesky dogs as far as the eye can see!"

Mum was already wishing she had never raised the subject.

"Look," she sighed "let's just forget about it for now – we'll talk about it some other time."

But she was too late – Dad was already working up a full head of steam.

"Well," he snorted "don't mind me. You go ahead and fill the whole house with dogs if you like!"

"Really George – there's no need to be like that…"

"How about bringing in a few dozen cats as well, just for good measure."

"Now you're being stupid."

"Ha!" Dad scoffed. "Me? Being stupid? For objecting to having my slippers filled with dog dirt?"

"Look George - I didn't mean..."

But Dad was already heading for the door.

"Well – I'll leave it up to you. In the meantime, I'm off to the *one* place in the whole wide world where I know for certain that I won't be plagued by pesky animals!"

And with these bitter words, he stomped from the room, pausing only to express his sincere hope that his wife wouldn't be bitten to death by fleas.

Stifling a scream of frustration, Mum watched him go; *if this carried on much longer, she'd end up in bed again with one of her migraines...*

Dad's intended destination was the garden shed. A good thirty yards from the house, it had often come in useful as a place of refuge, offering sanctuary and solitude whenever the outside world and all its worries got too much. The outside world and all its worries had been getting too much quite regularly of late, and for this reason, he had installed a comfy chair in which he planned to sit and while away an hour or so with a relaxing book. Half way down the garden path, crouched behind a large rhododendron bush, he encountered his daughter, Martha. She appeared, he noted, to be messing with the new garden hosepipe he had bought only last week – the very same hosepipe which she had been banned from touching under pain of death.

"Oh - hiya, Dad," she said, startled. She hadn't realized he was back from work just yet.

"What do you think you are doing?" Dad spoke tersely.

"Oh nothin' much," Martha shrugged. "I was a bit bored, so I jus' thought I'd help you and Mum by waterin' the garden."

This had Dad's blood pressure rocketing again.

"Oh you did, did you?" he barked. "I take it you've forgotten what happened the last time you 'helped' to water the garden?"

"Yes but…"

"The whole place was flooded. It was like something out of the Old Testament - all of my lettuces were completely drowned!"

"Yes Dad, but that was last week…"

"Look, Martha – I've had a very stressful day at work and don't need any more arguments right now. Why don't you go and do something useful, like finishing your homework, perhaps?"

And with this, in Martha's opinion, *outrageous* suggestion, he continued on his way to the sanctuary of his beloved shed. He had barely travelled a few paces, however, when a booming voice came from behind him.

"Guess what, Dad?" it bellowed. "I bought Ernie a new bone from Longbottom's today. I just gave it to him, but I'm not sure if he liked it."

"Oh?" Dad frowned. "Why ever not? Surely one rubber bone is the same as another."

"Not really," came the earnest reply. "It's pink, you see, and I don't think Ernie likes pink."

Chapter 6

In stating that she wasn't sure whether Ernie *liked* his new rubber bone, Martha had failed to grasp the true depths of the little dog's feelings towards it. Ernie didn't just *dislike* his new toy – he *hated* it more than he had ever hated anything in his whole life. As the contents of the package had revealed themselves, the state of wild excitement in which he had torn off the wrapping paper had quickly changed to one of stunned horror. *How could Martha do this to him? How could she be so cruel? Deliberately raising his hopes by putting a parcel the exact size and shape of his beloved bone in his basket, knowing full well that it contained this horrid pink imposter?*

With a *yip* of disgust, Ernie had turned on his heels and headed straight for the door, determined to put as much distance as possible between himself and the ghastly object. It was as he was tottering past the compost heap a few minutes later, still in a state of deep shock, that he was hailed by a familiar squeaky voice.

"You didn't manage to get it back then?"

"Sorry?" Ernie blinked at the mangy little mouse who was once again addressing him from its perch on the upturned wheelbarrow.

"Your bone." Montgomery trilled. "I'm assuming you didn't manage to get it back from that blighter next door."

"No," the little dog sighed. "He's got it in his kennel and thinks that it's his. There's no way I'll ever see that again…"

"Nonsense."

Ernie's heart rate quickened.

"W…What do you mean?" he stammered. *Was there still, even now, a chance he would get his beloved bone back?*

Montgomery hopped down from his wheelbarrow and scampered over to where the little dog stood, looking him squarely in the eye.

"I simply pointed out that your statement that you would never see your bone again was, in my opinion, nonsense."

"But…"

"I could just as easily have described it as *drivel, twaddle* or *poppycock…*"

"But Montgomery," Ernie protested "you told me yourself how scary Max was. I'm only small – how could I ever stand a chance against him?"

"Dear me," the little mouse scoffed "if everyone took that attitude, nobody would ever achieve anything. You know what King Robert the Bruce of Scotland told his troops shortly before they thrashed the English at the battle of Bannockburn, don't you?"

"No," Ernie replied truthfully.

"He said 'if at first you don't succeed, try, try and try again', and that is precisely what *we* must do."

Ernie fell silent for a moment whilst he considered this.

"That's all very well," he said, shaking his scruffy head doubtfully "but what about those teeth? And those claws?"

"Yes, yes, yes," Montgomery snorted with a dismissive wave of his tiny paw "he may indeed possess teeth and claws, but what he doesn't have is *brains!*"

Ernie's heart rate quickened further as sensed a glimmer of hope.

"What we must do," the mouse continued, warming to his theme "is come up with a cunning plan."

"Yes but…"

"It's quite simple. All we have to do is find a way to lure the beast from its lair…"

Ernie frowned as he pondered the mouse's words.

"Are you saying we should try to tempt Max away from his kennel?"

"Precisely," Mongomery grinned. "And with Max out of the picture, your bone will be there for the taking! Now listen carefully – here's what we'll do…"

*

In the shed, relaxing in the blissful comfort of his armchair, Dad let out a long, contented yawn as he finished the chapter of the detective novel he had been reading. Though he had almost reached the bit where the identity of the murderer was about to be revealed, the warm sun blazing through the shed windows had made him drowsy, so much so that he felt unable to continue without first having taken a restorative nap. At least he was guaranteed peace and quiet here in his dog-free place of refuge, and besides, he could always find out who the killer was when he woke up. And so, placing the book down on the shelf beside him, he closed his eyes and was fast asleep in a matter of moments.

*

Ernie crept cautiously into the porch where his bowl of Bingo's Beefy Bites lay, still untouched, from breakfast time. Had Martha been present, she would have been deeply relieved to witness him apparently tucking into his food with great gusto; what she would not have known, however, was that Ernie had not the slightest intention of *swallowing* the meaty snacks – instead, he was merely squeezing as many into his mouth as possible in order to transport them to a secret, unknown destination. His cheeks bulging, he trotted back out into the garden and off down the path, only to return a few minutes later in order to repeat the same action. A further two trips and the bowl was empty.

Down at the compost heap, Montgomery surveyed the little mound of food in the same critical way that a general might survey his stocks of ammunition.

"Hmmm," he pondered. "There's not *quite* as many Beefy Bites as I had anticipated, but hopefully there will be enough to get the job done."

"So what do we do now?" Ernie said, glancing dubiously at the soggy chunks of meat.

"You'd better leave this next part to me," the mouse replied. "Stealth is critical on a mission such as this, and my tiny size should enable me to move back and forth through enemy territory undetected."

"Yes but..."

"You, in the meantime, must adopt a defensive position behind that dustbin over there and await my signal."

Ernie was growing more confused by the minute.

"Signal?" he frowned. "What sort of signal?"

Montgomery scratched his tiny chin.

"Yes," he whispered. "That's a good point. It needs to be something subtle – something that will not arouse the suspicions of the enemy."

For a few seconds, he fell into a pensive silence.

"I've got it!" he exclaimed, jumping up with excitement. "I shall make a sound like the hoot of an owl."

"The hoot of an owl?" Ernie shook his head. "But that's ridiculous - it's the middle of the afternoon."

"Never mind that – it's what Special Forces always do in these situations. As soon as you hear the hooting sound, you'll know that the coast is clear and that it's time for you to move."

"Ok, but what if…"

"Shhh, my friend," Montgomery hissed "now listen carefully – here's what I need you to do when you hear the signal."

There followed a great deal of whispering as the mouse explained to Ernie in great detail what his role in the operation would be.

"Well?" he whispered, having concluded his piece. "Is that clear?"

"Yes," the little dog gulped. "At least, I think it is..."

"Very good," said the mouse. "Then I'll be off. If I do not return, please do your best to ensure that I have an honourable burial, and don't forget to inform my next of kin."

And before Ernie could reply, he hurriedly scooped a Bingo's Beefy Bite underneath each of his tiny armpits and vanished through the gap in the fence into next door's garden.

Chapter 7

Max awoke with a deep yawn. Having recovered from his encounter with the peculiar little dog from next door, he had soon drifted off into a pleasant slumber in the summer sunshine. Opening his eyes, he glanced sleepily around at his surroundings; *yes – his new rubber bone was still there – heaven help anyone who dared to try and pinch it again!* Satisfied that all was well, he rose to a sitting position and wiped a slobber of drool that was dripping from his chin with one massive paw. Max was a classic example of what is sometimes referred to as a *slobbery dog*, and he often awoke to find a pool of warm dribble in the area where he had been resting his head. Then he spotted something unusual; barely a yard from where he had been sleeping, there was what appeared to be a small chunk of meat. Rising stiffly on his haunches, he waddled forward to investigate. A quick sniff at the mysterious morsel was all that was required for a positive identification; *why – unless he* *was very much mistaken, it was a Bingo's Beefy Bite! He hadn't tasted one of those in ages!* Without further ado, he shot out his long, slobbery tongue and gobbled it up. Puzzled, but nevertheless pleasantly surprised by this unexpected treat, Max was turning to head back to his kennel when he spotted *another* one a few yards further down the path. Drooling as he had never drooled before, he took an eager step towards it, only to be reminded by the rattling of his chain that he was still attached to his kennel.

"Drat!" he muttered to himself. *"There's no way it'll stretch that far..."*

And yet when he turned around to look at the chain, Max was astonished to discover that it had been unfastened by a mysterious, unseen hand. An intelligent dog might, at this point, have sensed that there was something fishy going on, however, as we have already established, Max was *not* an intelligent dog. Far from it; he was a nincompoop of the first order. And so, with a greedy *woof* of delight, he trotted gamely off down the path and gobbled up the second chunk of meat in a single gulp. It tasted *even more delicious than the first one! But wait - what was this? Unless he was very much mistaken, there appeared to be a THIRD Beefy Bite a little further ahead down the path! Today wasn't turning out to be so bad after all...*

*

Hunkered down in his hidey-hole behind the dustbin, Ernie was growing more nervous with every passing moment. It seemed to him that Montgomery had been gone for hours and hours (though it was, in fact, somewhere in the region of four and a half minutes). *Where was he? Had Max got hold of him and chewed him into a fine mincemeat, just as he had promised?* Then he heard it – the sound of a large creature advancing through the undergrowth nearby. Peeping out from behind his dustbin, Ernie was astonished to see Max's bulky form advancing up the path towards him. *He must have forced his way through the gap in the fence! Was this all part of Montgomery's plan? If so, the mouse certainly hadn't told him about it...* Hardly daring to breathe, the little dog watched, keeping deathly still as the monster passed within inches of his hiding place, still hot on the trail of Bingo's Beefy Bites that led away up the path through the Miller's garden.

Barely had Max vanished from sight when Ernie was alerted by another sound. Cocking his right ear, he listened carefully... *Yes – there it went again – a sound that had a curious resemblance to the hoot of an owl; Montgomery's signal – it was time to act!* Plucking up all of the courage he could muster, the little dog crept from his hideout and scurried through the gap in the fence into next door's garden. But even as he began to make his way through the undergrowth towards Max's kennel, Ernie spotted a fatal flaw in the mouse's plan; *as soon as the trail of Beefy Bites ran out, Max would surely turn and head for home, and when he did, there was a distinct danger that they might bump into one another. It would not, Ernie feared, be a happy reunion, especially if he happened to be carrying the bone he had just pinched from the bulldog's kennel...*

"Montgomery, you nitwit," he cursed under his breath. "If only you'd thought of a way of keeping him busy for longer!"

Little did he know that the cunning little mouse had already seen to it that Max would be kept out of the picture for as long as was deemed necessary...

*

In the shed, Dad was dreaming deeply. It was a pleasant dream, one he had on a regular basis about a world in which there were no dogs – not a single one. Why this was, he did not know, nor did he care. All that mattered was that in this canine-free paradise, he was able to walk the streets and enjoy the scenery without having to keep his eyes constantly trained on the pavement for fear of stepping in something unpleasant. Equally, in this heavenly place, he was able to put on his slippers each morning with the carefree certainty that there would not be anything squidgy inside them. *But wait –*

what was that? A curious noise – a strange, growling sort of noise, just the kind of sound a dog would make. In his sleep, Dad twitched restlessly as the contented smile faded from his face.

"Grrrrrr!"

There it was again! But that was impossible – there WERE no dogs in this wondrous dreamland...

"Grrrrrrrrr!"

With a violent start, Dad sat bolt upright and opened his eyes. He blinked. And he blinked again. And again. *No – this could not be. He must be having a nightmare – yes that was it... He was still dreaming. There couldn't possibly be a large, ferocious-looking bulldog sitting in the shed with him... Could there?*

*

His heart beating double time, Ernie advanced warily up the path towards Max's kennel. As it came into view, he was relieved to see that all seemed quiet; *Montgomery's plan to lure the beast away had clearly worked.* And yet the closer he got, the more his spirits sank, for of his bone, his beloved, treasured bone, there was simply no sign. Unsure how to proceed, the little dog hesitated. *Should he abort the mission and settle for a new life with the Pink Imposter? Was it possible that, given the healing hands of time, he could learn to love it in the same way he had loved his old bone?* Ernie very much doubted it. *Still, it appeared that he had little choice. He had done his best – he was only sorry that his best had not been good enough...*

And so, with a sad sigh of resignation, he turned to head for home. Yet barely had he trotted a few paces, when something miraculous happened. It was, as we have previously mentioned, a still and sunny day, yet out of nowhere, a sudden gust of wind blew up, filling the little dog's senses with something all too familiar, a wonderful, delectable fragrance that almost made his heart burst with joy... *HIS BONE! Yet again, Ernie had picked up the scent of his bone!*

Spinning on his heels, he rushed back towards the kennel and dived in. Sniffling and snuffling like an undersized bloodhound, he followed the sweet scent further and further in until his little black nose came into contact with the back wall, and there, right in the darkest corner, hidden underneath a scruffy old blanket, he discerned a familiar knobbly shape. With a *yip* of glee, he seized the blanket in his teeth and hurled it to one side…

Chapter 8

Very, very slowly, his heart skipping to a salsa beat, Dad rose from his chair.

"S… Steady boy," he bleated. "Th…There's a good boy – nice doggy…"

And yet one glance at the snarling beast was enough to tell him that this particular specimen was anything *but* a 'nice doggy'; on the contrary, it was his worst nightmare come true.

"Grrrrrr!" replied Max.

Dad took a deep breath. The dog had, he noted to his dismay, taken up a strategic position between his armchair and the door of the shed, thereby blocking his only escape route. *Just try to stay calm* he told himself. *Don't make any sudden movements and everything will be ok.* With beads of cold sweat trickling down his brow, he glanced around. *There – in the corner – a stout broomstick. If he could only somehow reach it, he would at least have a means of defending himself.* Slowly, carefully, hardly daring to breathe, he extended his right arm…

"Grrrrrrr!" Max responded to the movement with another low growl, as if to warn his captive against trying any funny business. Though he had rather enjoyed following the trail of Bingo's Beefy Bites, he had not taken kindly to finding himself suddenly locked up in a small garden shed. And not only was he locked up in a small garden shed, but he was locked up in a small garden shed that contained a strange man - a strange man who persisted in calling him *nice doggy*, a name which no self-respecting canine will tolerate.

"N… N… Nice doggy," Dad repeated, adding insult to injury. *This is it* he thought to himself as his hand closed over the broom handle. *It's now or never…* Though not what anyone would describe as an agile man, he now moved with a speed that would stun any ninja, seizing the broomstick in a sudden, fluid motion. "Ha!" he shouted, triumphantly waggling his new-found weapon in the bulldog's face. "Not so fierce now are you?"

Max studied him quizzically. Whilst he didn't understand quite *why* the strange man was waving a broom at him, he sensed that he was not doing so in the spirit of friendship, and it was with this in mind that he took a menacing step forward and let out a thunderous bark that echoed around the four walls of the shed.

For Dad, whose feeble courage was already at breaking point, this proved to be the final straw. What little fighting spirit he had ever possessed vanished in that instant, the broom falling from his trembling hands with a loud clatter onto the wooden floor. He no longer cared about putting on a show of bravery. He no longer cared if anyone thought him a coward. All he cared about was getting as far away as he possibly could from this terrifying brute.

"Pleeeeeeese!" he wailed at the top of his voice. "Pleeeeeese help me!"

Unfortunately for Dad, the one thing that Max hated *even* more than being referred to as a *nice doggy*, was being shouted at for no apparent reason. He had, he felt, put up with this strange man's nonsense for quite long enough, and it was with this in the foremost of his thoughts that he took a menacing step forward and let out a bark that was at least twice as terrifying as his previous effort.

WOOOOOOOF! it boomed.

"Pleeeese!" Dad bawled as he tried in vain to claw his way out through the back wall. *"Someone... Anyone... Heeeeeeelp me!"*

*

Still clutching his precious bone tightly between clenched teeth, Ernie scuttled through the gap in the fence back into his own garden. Hardly daring to breathe, he glanced around. *Where was Max? Could he be lying in wait behind a bush, ready to ambush him?*

"Why, hello there!"

A shrill voice directly behind him sent him leaping skywards like a startled gazelle. Spinning round, Ernie was relieved to see the diminutive figure of Montgomery, perched as ever in his favourite spot on the upturned wheelbarrow.

"Hey," he scolded, dropping the bone at his feet. "What's with all the yelling? You nearly scared me to death!"

"Well that *is* charming," the mouse retorted warmly. "I see you've got your bone back, courtesy of my brilliant scheme, and that's all the thanks I get!"

"I'm sorry," Ernie sighed. "You just scared me, that's all. Thank you."

"You are *most* welcome," Montgomery grinned. "I am only glad to have been of service." He paused, noticing a distinct look of worry on the little dog's face.

"What's the matter?" he squeaked. "You've got your bone back, haven't you?"

"Yes," Ernie replied "but what about Max?"

"What about him?"

"Where is he?" the little dog glanced around nervously. "Didn't you lure him into this garden with those Beefy Bites?"

"Yes, yes, yes," Montgomery chuckled "but you needn't worry about him for the time being. Let's just say he's... He's been *detained*."

"Detained?" Ernie was increasingly baffled. "What do you mean, *detained*?"

"Never mind that," said the mouse. "All you need to know for now is that we needn't worry about Max for the time being. Ok?"

"I suppose so," Ernie agreed, though he sounded far from convinced.

"Good," Montgomery grinned, his voice suddenly taking on a business-like tone "and since my work here is done, perhaps now would be a suitable time to discuss payment for my services."

Ernie frowned.

"Payment?" he shook his head. "I don't understand - you never said anything about wanting money."

"No, no, no," the mouse chuckled. "Of *course* I don't want *money*. What good is money to a mouse of my age, or indeed of *any* age?"

Ernie was growing more confused by the minute.

"Then what *do* you want?" he implored.

"Well, since you ask," answered the mouse "what I would like is this…"

But I am afraid, reader, we will have to wait to find out what it was that Montgomery wanted, for at that precise moment, the conversation was rudely interrupted by a loud commotion from the vicinity of the garden shed.

Ernie pricked up his ears and listened intently. It was a curious, high-pitched squealing kind of noise, the sort of thing one might expect to hear from a startled pig.

"What the dickens was that?" Montgomery frowned. "How very odd. It sounded a bit like a damsel in distress – I never knew we had them in this part the world."

"No," Ernie replied thoughtfully. "I don't think it was that…" The sound was strangely familiar, reminding him of something he had heard only recently. *But what could it be?* Then it came to him; *the last time he had heard a squeal like that had been the other morning when Dad had put his foot in that slipper…*

"Then what was it then?" the mouse persisted. "It certainly sounded like a damsel in distress to me."

"No," the little dog replied, more firmly this time. "It wasn't a damsel in distress – it was Dad! Come on – *quick*, let's go and see what's wrong!"

*

By the time Ernie and Montgomery arrived at the shed, the din coming from the inside had reached a crescendo. The louder Dad yelled, the louder Max barked, and the louder Max barked, the louder Dad yelled, until the very walls of the small wooden building shook as though it had been hit by an earthquake.

"Hmm," Montgomery frowned, scratching his whiskery chin. "It seems as though I might have made a *slight* tactical error."

"What?" Ernie gasped. "Y… You mean you used the trail of Beefy Bites to lead Max into the shed?"

"Yes," the mouse cringed. "That was my plan…"

"And then you bolted the door…"

"Absolutely – it seemed like an excellent means of keeping him out of the way whilst our operation was in progress."

"But Dad was asleep in there!" Ernie shook his scruffy head in dismay. "You've really gone and messed things up now, haven't you?"

"Now just you look here," Montgomery retorted hotly. "How was I supposed to know he was sleeping in there? It's supposed to be a shed, not some sort of hotel! And besides…"

He was interrupted by another ear-splitting shriek from within the confines of the shed.

"Heeeeeeeeeeeelp!" it went.

"Look," Ernie yapped "we don't have time to argue. We've got to get him out, and quickly by the sounds of it!"

"Very well," cried the mouse. "Leave it to me!"

Ernie watched in amazement as his friend scurried like a spider, straight up the vertical wall of the shed, gripping the gaps between the planks of wood with his tiny paws. Arriving at the halfway mark, Montgomery halted, pausing only briefly to catch his breath before shimmying over to the large metal bolt that held the door firmly shut.

"You'll never get that open," Ernie hissed. "It's almost as big as you are!"

"Yes," came the reply. "I must admit it's a little on the stiff side."

As the mouse heaved and wrestled with the bolt for all he was worth Dad's cries from inside the shed grew ever more desperate.

"Come on!" Ernie urged, hopping up and down on his hind legs.

"Grrrr!" Montgomery grunted as he threw every last ounce of strength into his efforts.

We have, reader, already talked about *divine intervention*. Perhaps it now came to the mouse's aid, or perhaps he was just a great deal stronger than he looked, but either way, just when it seemed like all was lost, there was a groan and a grinding noise, and bolt shot aside with an almighty *thunk*.

"Help!" Montgomery cried as he was catapulted unceremoniously into the nearby compost heap, where he landed with an earthy *PLOP!*

Ernie, however, had more pressing matters on his mind; wide eyed with terror, he watched, rooted to the spot as, with a creak that sent shivers down his spine, the shed door slowly swung open...

Chapter 9

The scene confronting Ernie as he peered into the shed was the sort of thing a television news reporter might describe as a 'tense standoff.' In one corner, having retrieved his broomstick, Dad was brandishing it in the same way that a Zulu warrior might brandish a spear. Max, meanwhile, with his back to the door and oblivious to Ernie's presence, appeared to be stuck in something of a dilemma; his enemy, like Davy Crockett at the Alamo, was cornered with no means of escape, yet there was something about the menacing way in which Dad was waving that broom that gave him pause for thought.

Unsure what to do, Ernie was wondering whether to run to fetch Martha when Dad spotted him through the open door.

"Ernie," he gibbered in a strangled sort of voice. "Ernie please – you've got to help me!"

The little dog looked at him with mixed feelings. Though he sympathised with the man's plight, he could not help but remember some of the hurtful things that Dad had said in the aftermath of the slipper incident. He had, Ernie recalled, employed a series of fruity words and phrases, many of which he had never heard before, and none of which are suitable to be reproduced in this, a book intended for the younger reader.

"Please!" Dad repeated. "L… Look Ernie – I'm sorry about that business with the slipper. It was my fault – it was stupid of me to leave them lying there on the living room floor like that."

Ernie responded with a haughty *ruff* of agreement. *He knew that Dad would see sense sooner or later…*

"S… So how about we forget all about it, eh?" the stricken man continued. "Let bygones be bygones and all that? Perhaps we could…"

WOOOOOOF!

His voice was drowned out by another thunderous bark from Max.

For Dad, this was simply too much. "Pleeeeeese," he wailed. "Ernie - you can come into the house *every single night!* You can use my slippers as a toilet if you like! You can do *anything* you want, just *please* help me!"

Ernie cocked his ear with interest; this was *much* more like the sort of thing he wanted to hear. Indeed, the generosity of Dad's offer was such that he quickly decided that he would do everything in his power to help. The only question was what, exactly, could a little dog of his small stature do, faced with a monster like Max? As he saw it, the one thing which stood in his favour was the element of surprise; *if he could only sneak up on the huge dog undetected, Ernie felt confident he could give him a shock that he would not forget for a long, long time.* And so, hardly daring to breathe, he crept forward until his little black nose was barely an inch from Max's rear end.

*

Martha surveyed Dad's vegetable patch with a sense of deep satisfaction. *Yes, he might have said something about her not*

*playing with the hose or watering his
lettuces, but he couldn't really have meant
it. Anyway - that had been almost an hour
ago, and it was such a hot, sunny day that it
surely wouldn't hurt just to give them a
teensy weensy drop. Besides, she was very,
very, VERY bored, and he was always
telling her to make herself useful...* And so,
unable to resist the allure of the brand new
high-powered hose, Martha had diligently
set to work. To begin with, she had indeed,
watered his precious lettuces sparingly,
however this water had quickly drained
away into the soil, leaving her (as she saw it)
with little option but to add a *teensy weensy*
bit more. This pattern of events had
continued until, by the time she finally
replaced the hose in its holder, Dad's
vegetable patch bore a striking resemblance
to Lake Windermere. Or Lake Michigan, if
you happen to be reading this in the United
States.

"Mmm," she pondered to herself. "I
wonder if his tomatoes in the greenhouse are
ok. I 'spect they could do with a drop of

water too." And so off she went down the garden path, dragging the hose behind her.

*

If Max's previous barks had been notable for their loudness, they were mere whispers compared to the ear-splitting howl of agony that he emitted when Ernie's razor sharp teeth clamped firmly down onto his right buttock. With a *YOOOOOWL!* that could be heard in several adjoining counties, he blundered out of the shed, bucking and rearing like an Arab stallion in a frantic bid to dislodge his tormentor. Ernie, however, was equally determined *not* to be dislodged. As he saw it, the longer he could remain attached to the monster's hind quarters, the longer he would be safe from those terrible fangs, and it was with this foremost in his thoughts that he responded to the bucking and rearing by biting down ever harder.

YOOOOOOWL! Max roared again as he began to spin like a top, trying ever more desperately to shake off his attacker. Still, Ernie hung on for dear life, yet he did so

with a sinking heart; as the spinning grew
ever faster, so he felt the grip of his jaws
weakening until, with a final *yip* of dismay,
he found himself sailing through the air,
finally coming to rest with a juicy *SPLAT* in
the compost heap.

"Oof!" came a squeaky voice from
somewhere underneath him. "Watch what
you're doing!" The voice, of course,
belonged to Montgomery; having landed in
the compost heap but a few minutes earlier,
the unfortunate mouse had only just, with
great difficulty, managed to dig his way out
of the mud, when he found himself being
driven like a tack beneath the stinking
surface once again.

But Ernie had no time for apologies.
Dusting himself off, he saw to his horror
that Max was already bearing down on him,
snarling with rage. Pausing only to let out a
brief *yip* of alarm, he shot off up the garden
path as fast as his little legs would carry
him, with the bulldog in hot pursuit. The
sound of thundering feet and heavy
breathing behind him told him that his
enemy was quickly gaining ground; *if only*

he could make it to the house, perhaps Mum would be able to save him. She was always much braver than Dad in situations like this…

*

Having arrived at the greenhouse, Martha was reaching for the door handle when she became aware of a strange commotion down at the bottom of the garden. Frowning, she cocked her head and listened. It was a frantic yapping sort of a sound, the kind of noise that a small dog in peril might make, interspersed at regular intervals with the deep booming bark of a much larger specimen. One thing was for sure - whatever it was that was making the commotion was heading her way…

"Ernie!" Martha gasped, her eyes widening as, rounding the bend like a greyhound on a racetrack, the little dog hove into view, his little stumpy legs hammering away for all they were worth. Breathing down his neck, teeth bared, eyes ablaze with fury, there came another, much larger dog, one she had never seen before. Whereas Martha's eyes had initially widened, they now narrowed as her freckled face fixed itself into a look of grim resolve. *So – this horrid brute thinks he's going to hurt Ernie, does he? She would soon see about that...*

*

As he rounded the bend, with the bulldog snapping at his heels, Ernie's life flashed before him. Though he had run as he had never run before, his stumpy little legs had simply not been up to the task. He was a spent force, and any second now, he knew, he would feel the crunch of those terrible jaws upon his person. *Only a miracle could save him now...*

Closing on his prey, Max let out a snarl of triumph. Like most bullies, he was, in his heart of hearts, a coward. Had Ernie been even half his size, the bite on the bottom would have been enough to send him fleeing back to his own garden with little more than a whimper; as it was, he was relishing the prospect of teaching this annoying little pipsqueak a thing or two. It came as a nasty surprise to Max, therefore, when, at the very moment when his victim was almost within his grasp, he was blasted in the face at point-blank range by a raging jet of ice-cold water. The shock as it surged straight up his nostrils and into his mouth was enough to stop him dead in his tracks, just as surely as if he had run into a brick wall.

"Go on!" a voice bellowed through the watery haze. "Get out of here, unless you want some more!"

Choking and spluttering, not knowing what on earth had hit him, Max staggered back a few steps. If there was one thing he *did* know at that particular moment, it was that he did *not* want another blast of that ice-cold water. And so it was with a feeble whimper of surrender that he turned on his tail and fled off down the garden path as fast as his soggy legs would carry him.

"There's a good boy," Martha grinned, flinging the hose to one side and scooping a very grateful Ernie up into her arms. "Did that horrible dog frighten you? Well – I don't think he'll be coming round here again!"

For a few seconds, Ernie snuggled against the little girl, relieved to be back in the safety of her arms. Then a disturbing thought occurred to him; *his bone! He had dropped it somewhere down near the shed moments before he had bitten Max on the bottom. Max had just fled in that very direction. What if he saw it lying on the ground and picked it up? Everything he and Montgomery had worked for would have been in vain!*

With a yip of dismay, he wriggled free of Martha's grip and sped off down the garden path like a whippet.

"Hey!" she yelled. "Ernie – wait!"

But her cries fell on deaf ears. All that Ernie could think about was his beloved bone and he would not rest until it was safely back in his possession…

Chapter 10

Down in the shed, Dad continued to cower. *Sure, Ernie had distracted the big dog, but for how long?* However hard he tried, he couldn't imagine Martha's pet putting up enough of a fight to detain the brute for more than a few seconds, and then what? *Knowing his luck, it would be back, roosting in the shed with him before he knew it - that was what...* And so, with this fear foremost in his thoughts, he had set about feverishly barricading the shed door from the inside with everything he could lay his hands on. Lawnmowers, stepladders, pots of paint – all were used to form a formidable defensive barrier to keep the monster at bay until the Royal Marines (or, for that matter, Mum) came to his rescue. *But wait? What was this? There was something outside – something rattling the door, trying to get in...*

"Nooooo," he shrieked "you'll never take me alive!

The rattling stopped.

"Dad?" Martha sounded puzzled. "Is that you?"

Cautiously, hardly daring to believe his ears, Dad approached the shed door.

"M… Martha?" he called in what can only be described as a broken sob. "Is that you?"

"Yes," a voice boomed through the woodwork. "'Course it is. What are you doing in there? I can't open the door."

"Is… Is it gone?" came the husky reply.

Martha frowned.

"Is what gone?" she said, growing impatient.

"The big dog. Is the big dog gone?"

Martha's frown turned into a grin. Suddenly everything had become clear. *If she played her cards right, she would easily be able to turn this situation to her advantage…*

"Oh yes," she replied "it's gone. You needn't worry – Ernie chased it away."

There followed a great deal of clattering and cursing, accompanied by the sound of heavy objects being dragged aside as the barricade was dismantled. Seconds later, the door creaked open and Dad's head appeared. Wild-eyed and white as a sheet, he reminded Martha of a zombie she had seen in a recent episode of *Scooby Doo*. Grinning from ear to ear, she stood back and watched with mild amusement as he tottered gingerly out into the open, his eyes darting from right to left all the while, as though scarcely able to believe that the ferocious brute had truly been put to flight. It was only after several minutes of tottering, as the mists of terror gradually began to clear, that Dad became aware that his daughter was talking to him.

"So I 'spect you must be feeling pretty guilty about being so mean to Ernie after everything he's done," she was saying. "I 'spect you'll be keen to show him how grateful you are."

Dad goggled at her in bewilderment before transferring his gaze towards the compost heap where a familiar little dog could be observed gnawing with great relish on a yellow rubber bone. Had he looked more closely, he might have noticed that, between gnaws, it appeared to be engaged in an earnest conversation with a small, rather mangy-looking mouse.

"B… B… But…" he gibbered, turning back to his daughter. "I… I mean… *how* did he chase it away?"

"Never mind that," Martha grinned "he just did. Ernie's only small, but he's a lot tougher than he looks, you know."

"Yes but…"

"How about you start by saying 'sorry'?" the little girl continued forcibly.

"Sorry? But…" He gave Martha a pleading look, only to see her freckled features set in that familiar look of steely determination.

"I… I'm sorry, Ernie," he called over to the compost heap in a strangled sort of voice.

"Good," Martha beamed. "Now – let's all go and have some tea, and we can have a nice chat about when he'll be allowed back in the house…"

*

"Right then," said Martha as she guzzled down her last spoonful of desert. "I'm glad that's all settled. Can I leave the table now? I'm off to check if Ernie's ok."

"Yes," Mum nodded with a smile. "Don't be too long, though, because you've homework to finish before bedtime."

"Homework?" Martha turned to direct a fierce scowl at her mother.

"Yes – Have you forgotten? You were supposed to write a diary about your day."

"Oh *that*?" the little girl shrugged. "That won't take long – nothing much has really happened today."

And with this, she left the room, oblivious to the sound of Dad choking violently on his apple crumble.

*

As expected, she found Ernie in his basket in the porch, chewing on his yellow rubber bone with an air of quiet satisfaction. Kneeling down, she was about to give him a friendly tickle behind his ear when a thought occurred to her; *his new pink bone was nowhere to be seen.* The last time she had seen it, it had been in his basket, yet it now appeared to have vanished into thin air.

"Ernie," she said, her eyes narrowing. "Where's your new pink bone?"

As she stroked his back, Martha felt a strong shudder course through his little body at the very mention of the reviled object.

"Where is it?" she repeated. "I understand if you don't like it, and I don't mind if you've hidden it, but I just want to know where it is."

Ernie, however, was deaf to her pleas. As far as he was concerned, the monstrous *Pretender to the Bone* had been suitably disposed of; it had passed from his life once and for all, and he wanted nothing more to do with it. And so, with a stubborn shrug, he assumed an expression of innocence and resumed his tender gnawing.

The mystery of the vanishing pink bone was not one which would have taxed Sherlock Homes. Indeed, Martha had barely set foot in the garden when its final resting place became blatantly obvious.

"Oh no!" she gasped, clutching her head in her hands. "Oh Ernie – how *could* you?"

For there, right in the middle of the front lawn, were signs that the little dog had been extremely busy whilst they had been having their evening meal. Determined that the ghastly abomination should never again see the light of day, he had dug deep, deeper than he had ever dug in his entire life, and Martha had an uneasy suspicion that Dad would not appreciate the resulting mountain of earth that had become a new, predominant feature of his lawn. She frowned, thinking hard. *If her father saw this, Ernie's standing in the Miller household would be forever ruined. He would, for want of a better expression be 'in the dog house.' Could the mysterious mountain of soil be passed off as a mole hill? Perhaps it could, except Dad would be sure to investigate the hole, and the minute he found that pink bone, Ernie would be banged to rights. Not even she, with all her persuasive powers, could persuade him that a mole had somehow entered their house, taken the pink bone from Ernie's basket and buried it in the middle of the front lawn. No – there was only one thing for it – she would have to act, and act fast...* And so, with a look of grim determination, Martha stomped off down to the shed to fetch a spade.

Just as Ernie had done before her, she dug, and she dug, and she dug some more, always casting nervous glances towards the house, dreading the sound of heavy footsteps approaching down the path. Fortunately for Martha, though she did not know it, there was a football game on the television that night which would keep Dad safely out of the picture for much of the evening. All around her, dusk was setting in, the skies darkening as a nearby blackbird tootled a final tune before turning in for the night. And still there was no sign of the bone... It was only when she was on the verge of giving up, cross, weary and coated from head to toe in mud, that she spotted a glimpse of pink shining up at her through the murk.

"Yes!" she yelled, sending the dozing blackbird fluttering skyward with a cry of alarm. Lying flat on her stomach, heedless to the vast quantities of soil on her face, clothes and in hair, Martha reached down into the void and grasped the bone in her grubby hand.

But what now? How could she dispose of the evidence? There was no point in taking it back to the house – Ernie simply would not tolerate it. Nor could she return it to the shop for a refund – Mr Longbottom had, after all, let her have it for free. Then a thought occurred to her; *that dog next door. It had seemed like a horrid creature, but maybe it was just lonely. Maybe it didn't have a kind owner who loved it as she did Ernie. Maybe it would appreciate a new rubber bone, even if it WAS a pink one...* And so, just as she had done a few short days ago, she drew back her right arm and, with the power and technique of an Olympic shot-putter, launched the bone high over the fence and into next-door's garden.

"There!" she grinned, rubbing her hands with satisfaction. "All sorted – now I s'pose I'd better get that hole filled in before Dad sees..."

Epilogue

Ernie and Martha were not the only ones who had been busy that evening. In a little hole in the ground underneath Dad's shed, Montgomery had also been working tirelessly. When he had earlier mentioned 'payment' for his services, all he had, in fact, wanted was a guarantee from Ernie that he would be allowed to set up home beneath the shed in the Miller's garden without fear of being evicted as he had been from his previous residence round at Old Mrs Wiseman's. Ernie, of course, had been more than happy to grant him his wishes, the little dog having high hopes of a long and happy friendship that would stretch far ahead into the future.

"Ah yes," the mouse sighed with deep satisfaction as he tucked himself into his tiny bed of straw. "This is just the place for me."

There is an old saying from the Scottish poet Robert Burns which suggests that "the best-laid plans of mice and men often go awry," meaning that, however carefully we plan something, there is still a chance that it could all go horribly wrong. As he nodded off to sleep that evening, Montgomery reflected that, whilst this may indeed be true with respect to mice and *men,* the best-laid plans of mice and *dogs* generally seemed to work out rather well...

*

An outsider peering into the living room of the Miller household that evening, would have witnessed what, at a glance, appeared to be a scene of perfect tranquillity and domestic bliss. In an armchair in the corner of the room, a man sat in his dressing gown and slippers, gazing at the television, showing no outward signs of the harrowing ordeal through which he had passed but a few short hours beforehand. Directly opposite him, reclining sleepily in a second armchair, a lady, also clad in a dressing gown, was apparently deeply absorbed in a paperback novel. On the big leather sofa nearest the fireplace, meanwhile, there lay a little girl in a purple nightie. And on her knee, gnawing contentedly on a yellow rubber bone whilst he watched the television, there nestled a small, brown, somewhat scruffy-looking dog. All in all then, as previously stated, a scene of tranquillity and domestic bliss. *Or was it?*

In actual fact, only three out of the four bodies present could be described as truly happy. Martha was happy because Ernie had once more been reinstated in his rightful position on her lap. Mum was happy simply because Martha was happy. And Ernie – what can we say about Ernie other than that he was in a state of unbridled, heavenly bliss. Not only was he back in the warmth of the living room, snug and warm on Martha's lap, but he had also been reunited with the one and only love of his life – his yellow rubber bone. *Could things get any better than this?*

But what of Dad? I hear you ask. Well, reader, as for Dad, he had decidedly mixed feelings about the day's events. Yes – he grudgingly accepted that Ernie had done him a favour by chasing the vicious dog away, however he only had Martha's word on this, and held sneaking suspicions that she may not have *quite* told the truth, the whole truth and nothing but the truth of the matter. In addition to this vague feeling that he had somehow been tricked, he was annoyed that Ernie's original crime of pooping in his slipper appeared to have been completely forgotten by the rest of the family. *What,* he asked himself, *was civilization coming to when such a heinous act could go unpunished?* It was in this dark and brooding frame of mind that, as the ten o'clock news ended, he rose stiffly from his chair and muttered something about heading up to bed for an early night, pausing only to cast a withering glance at the little girl and her dog as he headed out of the door.

*

In his kennel in next door's garden, Max closed his eyes with a sleepy sigh and thought about his day. Sure, it had started promisingly when he had found a yellow rubber bone in his garden. Although it had been dirty, chewed up and clearly past its sell-by date, he had never owned a rubber bone before and had been most delighted with his discovery. Following this, however, things had quickly taken a turn for the worst. The next thing he knew, he had awoken from his mid-morning nap only to find a horrid little dog attempting to steal it from him. Shortly after this, he had been lured from his home by a dastardly trick and locked up in a shed with a strange man who had, for reasons Max failed to understand, insisted on waving a broomstick in his face. As if that wasn't bad enough, he had then been bitten on the bottom by the very same wicked little dog that had earlier tried to steal his bone, the whole ordeal being rounded off with a jet of ice-cold water in the face. By the time he had returned to his kennel, Max had cut a sad, soggy and broken figure. *Why did everything in his life seem to turn out wrong? Why, oh why, couldn't something nice happen to him, just for once?*

But at that very moment, just when he had been wallowing in the deepest depths of despair, something nice *had* happened to him. As if sent from the Gods, a pink rubber bone had come hurtling out of nowhere and landed on the patio right in front of his very nose. Scarcely able to believe his eyes, Max had crept forward and given it a tentative sniff. It had *smelled* real. Then he had licked it. It had *tasted* real. It *was* real – his very own rubber bone! Furthermore, it wasn't a dirty, tatty old chewed-up thing like the one he'd found before – this was brand new! *Oh joy of joys – Lady Luck had found him at last!* As he drifted off to sleep, Max's last thought was that it perhaps wasn't such a bad world after all...

*

The next day dawned bright and fair. After a restless night, tormented by nightmares of fiendish, snarling dogs, Dad was nevertheless the first to awaken in the Miller household. Descending the stairs, he crossed the hall and, as was his usual practice, donned his slippers on his way through to the kitchen. But as he did so, he experienced the distinctly unpleasant sensation of something squelching between his toes…

"*MARTHA!*" he shrieked, tearing the slipper off as he hopped madly around the hallway. "*MARTHA!* Get down here at once! That blasted dog of yours has only gone and done it *again*!"

*

Through in the porch, awoken by the commotion out in the hallway, Ernie sat up in his basket. Cocking his head to one side, he listened with growing interest to Dad's rantings and ravings, which were soon joined by the sound of Martha's voice, rising in protest. Amidst the din, one word in particular kept cropping up; 'slippers'. For some strange reason, Dad seemed deeply unhappy about his slippers. Ernie gave his bone a thoughtful nibble. *What was the matter with the old so-and-so now? Surely he hadn't already forgotten that there were not one, but **two** parts to the deal they had struck down at the shed the previous* *afternoon.* The first, that Ernie should be allowed back into the house, Dad had duly honoured; the second, relating to the shared use of the tartan size-tens, he appeared to have forgotten completely! *Human beings,* the little dog concluded, *were a curious species; highly intelligent in many ways, but a little dumb in others.* With a sigh of anticipation, Ernie gave his beloved bone another tender nibble as he readied himself for what promised to be another interesting day with the Millers...

The End

Other titles by James Sutherland

Norbert

Norbert's Summer Holiday

Christmas with Norbert

Norbert to the Rescue!

Norbert's Spooky Night

Norbert – The Collection

Roger the Frog

The Further Adventures of Roger the Frog

The Tale of the Miserous Mip

Frogarty the Witch

Jimmy Black and the Curse of Poseidon

About the Author

James Sutherland was born in Stoke-on-Trent, England, many, many, many years ago. So long ago, in fact, that he can't remember a thing about it. The son of a musician, he moved around lots as a youngster, attending schools in the Isle of Man and Spain before returning to Stoke where he lurked until the age of 18. After gaining a French degree at Bangor University, North Wales, James toiled manfully at a variety of office jobs before making a daring escape through a fire exit, hell-bent on writing silly nonsense full-time. In his spare time, James enjoys hunting for slugs in the garden, chatting with his gold fish and frolicking around the house in his tartan nightie.

Visit www.jamessutherlandbooks.com for more information and all the latest news!